Finding Sammy

Little Stinker Series
Book 1

Dave Sargent was born and raised on a dairy farm in northwest Arkansas. When he began writing in 1990, he made a decision to dedicate the remainder of his life to encouraging children to read and write. He is very good with students and teachers alike. He and his wife Pat travel across the United States together. They write about animals with character traits. They are good at showing how animals act a lot like kids.

Finding Sammy

Little Stinker Series
Book 1

By Dave Sargent

Illustrated by Elaine Woodward

Ozark Publishing, Inc.
P.O. Box 228
Prairie Grove, AR 72753

Cataloging-in-Publication Data

Sargent, Dave, 1941–
    Finding sammy / by Dave Sargent ;
illustrated by Elaine Woodward. —Prairie
Grove, AR : Ozark Publishing, c2007.
    p. cm. (Little stinker series ; 1)

    "Be curious"—Cover.
    SUMMARY: Dave and his dog Tippy
find a den of baby skunks inside an old rock
wall. The little skunks come out of the wall
and start playing with him. One of the little
skunks is white.
    ISBN 1-59381-273-6 (hc)
          1-59381-274-4 (pbk)

    1. Skunks—Juvenile fiction.
2. Dogs—Juvenile fiction.
[1. Games—Fiction.]
I. Woodward, Elaine, 1956– ill.
II. Title. III. Series.

    PZ7.S243Fi 2007
    [Fic]—dc21   2005906107

Printed in the United States of America

iv

Inspired by

a den of baby skunks Dave found when he was seven years old.

Dedicated to

my little stinkers who live beside me, my granddaughters: Amber, April, Ashley and Faith London.

Foreword

Dave and his dog Tippy find a den of baby skunks inside an old rock wall. The little skunks come out of the wall and start playing with Dave. One is solid white.

Contents

One   School Is Out!   1

Two   Playing Games   7

Three   Finding Sammy   13

Four   Skunk Facts   18

If you'd like to have Dave Sargent, the author of the Little Stinker Series, visit your school free of charge, call: 1-800-321-5671.

One

School Is Out!

"Yahoooo!" I yelled and sailed out the door the instant the bell rang. School was out and I was ready to go home. I hurried to the bus and took my place in the back.

It was a long way to my stop, and the bus driver wanted everyone who got off last to sit in the back.

The long ride home took around an hour and fifteen minutes. All the roads were dirt and full of potholes. The ride was bumpy. The bus had to go slow. I was anxious to get home. I knew my dog would be waiting.

By the time we got to my stop there were only three kids left on the bus.

I jumped off the bus and took off in a dead run toward home. It was a little over a half mile to the house. But since I was always anxious to get home, I didn't really mind the walk.

I lived way out in the country. Our nearest neighbor lived more than a mile away. I had no one to play with. So you can imagine how I felt when I got near the halfway point and saw Tippy, my ole dog, running up the road to meet me.

I yelled, "Come on, Tippy!"

When we reached each other I dropped to my knees and threw my arms around Tippy. He licked my face all over. You'd think we hadn't seen each other for weeks.

Tippy and I ran side by side the rest of the way home.

The weather was too nice to be inside. It was early spring, the sun was shining, and it was nice and warm outside. I ran into the house to change my clothes, and Tippy waited by the front door.

Two

Playing Games

I put on my work clothes and sailed out the front door.

As Tippy and I ran across the yard, I heard Mom say, "Don't forget, Dave! It'll be chore time soon!"

"Okay, Mom," I yelled as Tippy and I made our way to the woods.

When Tippy and I got to the woods, we slowed down. Just a short way off there was an old rock fence. I stopped at the end of the fence and sat down beside Tippy.

I had helped build this fence. My brothers and I had picked up rocks out of our fields so we could plant corn and other vegetables. We had stacked the rocks carefully to build the fence.

We rested for a few minutes, and then I looked at Tippy. "You want to play Cowboys and Indians, Tippy?"

Tippy wagged his tail. That was a "yes" to me.

I said, "We'll be the Indians, Tippy. We'll slip up on the cowboys. They're resting their horses just down the hill on the other side of this fence. Come on, Boy."

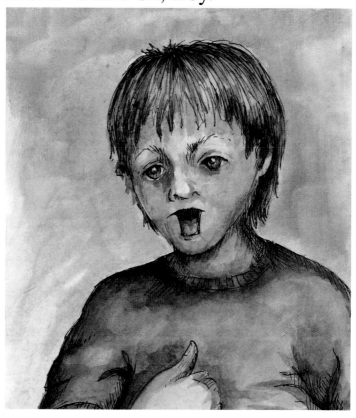

I dropped to the ground and began crawling on my belly next to the rock fence.

I whispered, "Now, we have to be real quiet, Tippy." He looked at me and wagged his tail. That meant he understood.

Tippy flattened himself on the ground and crawled right alongside me. We played together all the time, and he knew the rules.

Three

Finding Sammy

We had crawled just a few feet when I heard a strange screeching sound coming from inside the rock fence. I stopped and started looking back in between the rocks.

I saw a whole bunch of little bitty eyes.

I turned and looked at Tippy. He had moved several feet away. I said, "Come on, Tippy." He crawled even farther away.

I looked back at those little eyes. I started to stick my hand in and pull out one of whatever was in there.

My hand got closer and closer, but then I jerked it back. I suddenly realized that there might be a bunch of snakes in there. That might be why Tippy had moved so far away.

I looked around and found a stick about three feet long. I moved several feet from the fence, then lay down on my stomach and pushed the stick back in between the rocks.

I could feel something bumping against the stick. And then I felt something chewing on it. I began pulling the stick slowly out of the hole. Low and behold, hanging onto the end of that stick for dear life was a baby skunk about two inches tall.

I reached over to touch the little skunk. He jumped on my hand and began nibbling on my fingers.

I glanced back at the hole just in time to see another little skunk stick his head out. Then he pulled back inside.

I started playing with the little skunk that was chewing on all my fingers. Suddenly, another baby skunk jumped on my hand and began playing.

It wasn't long until there were eight of them playing with me.

I was having so much fun that I forgot about the time.

Four

Skunk Facts

The striped skunk has a black coat with two white stripes down the back and one white stripe going up the forehead. These stripes warn other animals to stay away.

A skunk is the size of a house cat. A skunk's eyes and ears are small. It cannot see well but its sense of hearing is good.